العَفاريتِ الصِّغارُ والاسْكافِيُّ

The Elves and The Shoemaker

retold by Henriette Barkow

illustrated by Jago

Arabic translation by Wafa' Tarnowska

Mantra Lingua

كانَ يا ما كانَ في قَديمِ الزَّمانِ إسكافيٌّ يَعيشُ مَعَ زَوْجَتِهِ ويَعْمَلُ بِجَهْدٍ شَديدٍ. لكنَّ موضةَ الأزْياءَ كانَتْ تَتبدَّلُ ولَمْ يَعُدِ النّاسُ بَعدَ ذلِكَ يشترونَ أَحْذيَةَ الإسْكافيِّ حتّى صارَ أَفقَرَ وأَفْقَرَ؛ وفي النِّهايَةِ لَمْ يَبْقَ لَدَيْهِ مِنَ الجِلدِ إلا ما يَكفِي لِصُنعِ زَوْجِ أحذيَةٍ واحِدٍ فقطْ.

Once there lived a shoemaker and his wife. He worked hard, but fashions changed and people didn't buy his shoes any more. He became poorer and poorer. In the end he only had enough leather to make one last pair of shoes.

قُصّ ... قُصّ! قَصَّ الاسْكافِيُّ الجِلدَ
على شكْلِ حذائَيْنِ.

Snip, snip! He cut out the shape
of two shoes.

تَرَكَهُما على دَكَّةِ العَمَلِ لِيبْدَأَ بِخياطَتِهِما
في الصَّبَاحِ.

He left them on the workbench ready
to start sewing in the morning.

وعِنْدَمَا نَزَلَ إِلى دُكَّانِهِ في اليَوْمِ التَّالي وَجَدَ ... زَوْجَ أَحْذِيَةٍ رَائِعًا يَنْتَظِرُهُ.
رَفَعَهُمَا وتَفَحَّصَهُمَا ورأى أَنَّ كُلَّ قُطْبَةٍ كانتْ مُخَيَّطَةً بِإِتْقَانٍ فَتَسَاءَلَ:
"يَا تُرَى مَنْ هو صَانِعُ هَذِهِ الأَحْذِيَةْ؟"

The next day, when he came downstairs, he found... a beautiful pair of shoes.
He picked them up and saw that every stitch was perfectly sewn.
"I wonder who made these shoes?" he thought.

في اللَّحْظَةِ نَفْسِهَا دَخَلَت امْرأَةٌ وقالتْ: "هذا زَوْجُ الأَحْذِيَةِ رائِعٌ جِداً.
ما هو سِعْرُهُ؟"

أَخْبرَهَا الاسْكافِيُّ بالسِّعْرِ فَأَعْطَتْهُ ضِعْفَ ما طَلَبَهُ مِنَ المَالِ.

Just then a woman came in to the shop. "Those shoes are gorgeous,"
she said. "How much are they?"
The shoemaker told her the price but she gave him twice the money
he had asked for.

أَصبَحَ لَدى الاسْكافِيِّ مالاً كافياً لِيَشْتَرِيَ طَعَاماً وَبَعْضَ الجِلْدِ لِيَصنَعَ زوجَيْ أَحْذِيَةٍ آخرَيْنِ.

Now the shoemaker had enough money to buy food and some leather to make two pairs of shoes.

قُصّ، قُصّ! قُصّ، قُصّ!
قَصَّ الاسْكافِيُّ الجِلْدَ على شَكْلِ أربَعَةِ أحذِيَةٍ.

Snip, snip! Snip, snip!
He cut out the shapes of four shoes.

تَرَكَهَا على دَكَّةِ العَمَلِ لِيَبْدَأ خِيَاطَتَهَا
في الصَّبَاحِ.

He left them on the workbench ready
to start sewing in the morning.

وعِنْدَمَا نَزَلَ إِلى دُكَّانِهِ في اليَوْمِ التَّالي وَجَدَ ... زَوْجَيْ أَحْذِيَةٍ رَائِعَيْنِ

فتَسَاءَلَ: "يا تُرى مَنِ الذي صَنَعَ هذِهِ الأَحْذِيَةَ؟"

وفي اللَّحْظَةِ نفْسِهَا دَخَلَ الدُّكَّانَ رَجُلٌ وامْرَأَةٌ. قَالَ الرَّجُلُ: "اُنظُري إِلى هَذِهِ الأَحْذِيَةِ."

أَجَابَتِ المَرْأَةُ: "هُنَاكَ زَوجٌ لَكَ وزَوجٌ لي."

سَأَلَتِ المَرْأَةُ الاسْكَافِيَّ: "كَم سِعْرُهَا؟"

أَخْبَرَهُمَا بِالسِّعْرِ لكنَّهُمَا أَعْطَيَاهُ ضِعْفَ ما طَلَبَهُ.

The next day, when he came down the stairs, he found... two beautiful pairs of shoes.
"I wonder who made these shoes?" he thought.
Just then a couple came in to the shop. "Look at those shoes," said the man.
"There is one pair for you and one pair for me. How much are they?" asked the woman.
The shoemaker told them the price, but they gave him twice the money he had asked for.

أَصْبَحَ لَدَى الاسْكافِيِّ مالاً كافِياً لِيَشْتَرِيَ طَعاماً أَكْثَرَ
وبَعْضَ الجِلْدِ لِيَصْنَعَ أَرْبَعَةَ أَزْواجٍ أَحْذِيَةٍ.

Now the shoemaker had enough money to buy more food and some leather to make four pairs of shoes.

قُصّ، قُصّ! قُصّ، قُصّ! قُصّ، قُصّ! قُصّ، قُصّ!

قَصَّ الاسْكافِيُّ الجِلْدَ على شَكْلِ ثَمانِيَةِ أَحْذِيَةٍ

وتَرَكَهَا على دَكَّةِ العَمَلِ لِيَبْدَأَ خِيَاطَتَهَا في الصَّبَاحِ.

Snip, snip! Snip, snip! Snip, snip! Snip, snip!
He cut out the shapes of eight shoes. He left them on
the workbench ready to start sewing in the morning.

عِنْدَمَا نَزَلَ إِلَى دُكَّانِهِ فِي اليَوْمِ التَّالِي وَجَدَ ... أَرْبَعَةَ أَزْوَاجٍ أَحْذِيَةٍ رَائِعَةٍ أُخْرَى

فَتَسَاءَلَ: "يَا تُرَى مَنِ الَّذِي صَنَعَ هَذِهِ الأَحْذِيَةَ؟"

وَفِي اللَّحْظَةِ نَفْسِهَا دَخَلَتْ عَائِلَةٌ إِلَى الدُّكَّانِ. قَالَ الصَّبِيُّ: "آه، اُنْظُرُوا إِلَى هَذِهِ الأَحْذِيَةِ!"

أَجَابَتِ الفَتَاةُ: "هُنَاكَ زَوْجُ أَحْذِيَةٍ لِي وَزَوْجٌ لَكَ."

وَقَالَ الصَّبِيُّ: "وَزَوْجُ أَحْذِيَةٍ لِأُمِّي وَزَوْجٌ لِأَبِي."

وَسَأَلَ الوَالِدَانِ: "كَمْ سِعْرُهَا؟"

وَأَخْبَرَهُمُ الاسْكَافِيُّ بِالسِّعْرِ لَكِنَّهُمْ أَعْطَوْهُ ضِعْفَ مَا طَلَبَهُ مِنَ المَالِ.

The next day when he came down the stairs he found... four beautiful pairs of shoes.
"I wonder who made these shoes?" he thought.
Just then a family came in to the shop. "Wow! Look at those shoes!" said the boy.
"There is a pair for you and a pair for me," said the girl.
"And a pair for mum and a pair for dad," said the boy.
"How much are they?" asked the parents. The shoemaker told them the price, but they gave him twice the money he had asked for.

وهكَذا في كُلِّ مَسَاءٍ كَانَ الاسْكَافِي يَقُصُّ الجِلْدَ لِأَحْذِيَةٍ جَدِيدَةٍ، وفي كُلِّ صَبَاحٍ كَانَ يَجِدُ أَحْذِيَةً جَمِيلَةً مَدْرُوزَةً بِإِتْقَانٍ مِنْ جَمِيعِ الأَشْكَالِ والمَقَاسَاتِ:ومنْها أَحْذِيَةٌ لِلرِجَالِ وأَحْذِيَةٌ لِلنِسَاءِ وأَحْذِيَةٌ لِلصّبْيَانِ وأَحِذِيَةٌ لِلبَنَاتِ وأَحْذِيَةٌ كَبِيرَةٌ وأَحْذِيَةٌ صَغِيرَةً وأَحْذِيَةٌ لِلشِّتَاءِ وشَبَاشِبُ الْبَيْتِ. وَقَدْ كَانَتْ هَذِهِ الأَحْذِيَةُ أَحْسَنَ أَحْذِيَةٍ فِي الْبَلَدِ.

Now every evening the shoemaker would cut out the leather for new shoes and every morning there would be perfectly stitched beautiful shoes of all shapes and sizes - shoes for men and shoes for women, shoes for boys and shoes for girls, big shoes and small shoes, boots and slippers. They were the best shoes in the land.

وبَدَأَتِ اللَيَالِي تَطُولُ وَتَبْرُدُ فَجَلَسَ الاسْكافيُّ يُفَكِّرُ وِيَتَسَاءَلُ مَنْ هُوَ صَانِعُ هَذِهِ الأَحْذِيَة. قُصّ ... قُصّ! قَصَّ الاسْكافي الجِلْدَ للأَحْذِيَة.

قَالَ لِزَوْجَتِه: "عِنْدِي فكرةٌ، لِنَسْهَرَ كَيْ نَكْتَشِفَ مَنِ الذي يَصْنَعُ أَحْذِيَتَنا."

فَاخْتَبَأَ الاسْكافيُّ وَزَوْجَتُهُ وَرَاءَ رُفُوف الدُّكان. عِنْدَمَا دَقَّتِ السَاعَةُ الثَانِيَةَ عَشَرَةَ مُنْتَصَفَ اللَيْلِ بالضَّبْطِ، ظَهَرَ رَجُلَانِ صَغِيرَانِ.

As the nights became longer and colder the shoemaker sat and thought about who could be making the shoes.
Snip, snip! Snip, snip! The shoemaker cut out the leather for the shoes.
"I know," he said to his wife, "let's stay up and find out who is making our shoes." So the shoemaker and his wife hid behind the shelves.
On the stroke of midnight, two little men appeared.

وجَلَسَا الرَجُلَانِ الصَغيرَانِ عَلى دَكَّةِ العَمَلِ وَأَخَذا يَخيطَانِ، خِطْ، خِطْ، خِطْ.

They sat at the shoemaker's bench.
Swish, swish! They sewed.

طَقْ، طَقْ، طَقْ، طَرَقَا بِالمِطْرَقَة.
كَانَتْ أَصابِعُهُما تَعْمَلُ بِسُرْعَةٍ كَبيرَةٍ حَتَّى كَادَ الاسْكَافِيُّ أَنْ لا يُصَدِّقَ عَيْنَيْهِ.

Tap, tap! They hammered in the
nails. Their little fingers worked
so fast that the shoemaker
could hardly believe his eyes.

خِطْ، خِطْ! طَقْ، طَقْ! لَمْ يَتَوَقَّفَا إِلا عِنْدَمَا أَصْبَحَتْ كُلُّ قِطْعَةٍ مِنَ الجِلْدِ حِذَاءً. ثُمَّ قَفَزَا عَنْ دَكَّةِ العَمَلِ وَهَرَبَا.

Swish, swish! Tap, tap! They didn't stop until every piece of leather had been made into shoes.
Then, they jumped down and ran away.

قَالَت الزَّوْجَةُ: "آهًا لِهَذَيْنِ الرَجُلَيْنِ الصَّغيرَيْنِ! لا بُدَّ أَنَّهُمَا يَبْرُدَانِ فِي هَذِهِ الثِّيَابِ البَالِيَة. لَقَدْ سَاعَدَانا بِعَمَلِهِمَا الجَهِيدِ وهُمَا لا يَمْلِكَانِ شَيْئًا. يَجِبُ أَن نُقَدِّمَ لَهُمَا شَيْئًا."

سَأَلَ الاسْكَافِيُّ: "مَا الذي يَجِبُ أَنْ نَفْعَلَهُ بِرَأْيِك؟"

قَالَت الزَّوْجَةُ: "عِنْدِي فِكْرَةٌ، سَأَصْنَعُ لَهُمَا ثِيابًا مُدَفِّئَةً لِيَلْبَسَاهَا."

وقَالَ الاسْكَافِيُّ: "وَسَأَصْنَعُ لَهُمَا أَحْذِيَةً لِأَرْجُلِهِمَا البَارِدَةِ الحَافِيَةِ."

"Oh, those poor little men! They must be so cold in those rags," said the wife.
"They have helped us with all their hard work and they have nothing.
We must do something for them."
"What do you think we should do?" asked the shoemaker.
"I know," said the wife. "I will make them some warm clothes to wear."
"And I will make them some shoes for their cold, bare feet," said the shoemaker.

في الصَّبَاحِ التَّالِي لَمْ يَفْتَحِ الاسْكَافِي وَزَوْجَتُهُ دُكَّانَهُمَا كَالعَادَةِ. أَمْضَيَا النّهَارَ كُلَّهُ يَعْمَلانِ وَلَكِنْ لَيْسَ بِبَيْعِ الأَحْذِيَةِ.

The next morning the shoemaker and his wife didn't open the shop as usual. They spent the whole day working but it wasn't selling shoes.

تَكْ، تَكْ، تَكْ!

حَاكَتِ الزَوْجَةُ سِتْرَتَيْنِ صَغِيرَتَيْنِ.

تَكْ، تَكْ، تَكْ!

حَاكَتْ أَرْبَعَةَ جَوارِبَ صوفِيَّةً.

Clickety, click! The shoemaker's
wife knitted two small jumpers.
Clickety, click! She knitted two
pairs of woolly socks.

خط، خط! خط، خط!

خَاطَتْ بَنْطَلونَيْنِ مُدَفِّئَيْنِ.

Swish, swish! Swish, swish!
She sewed two pairs of warm trousers.

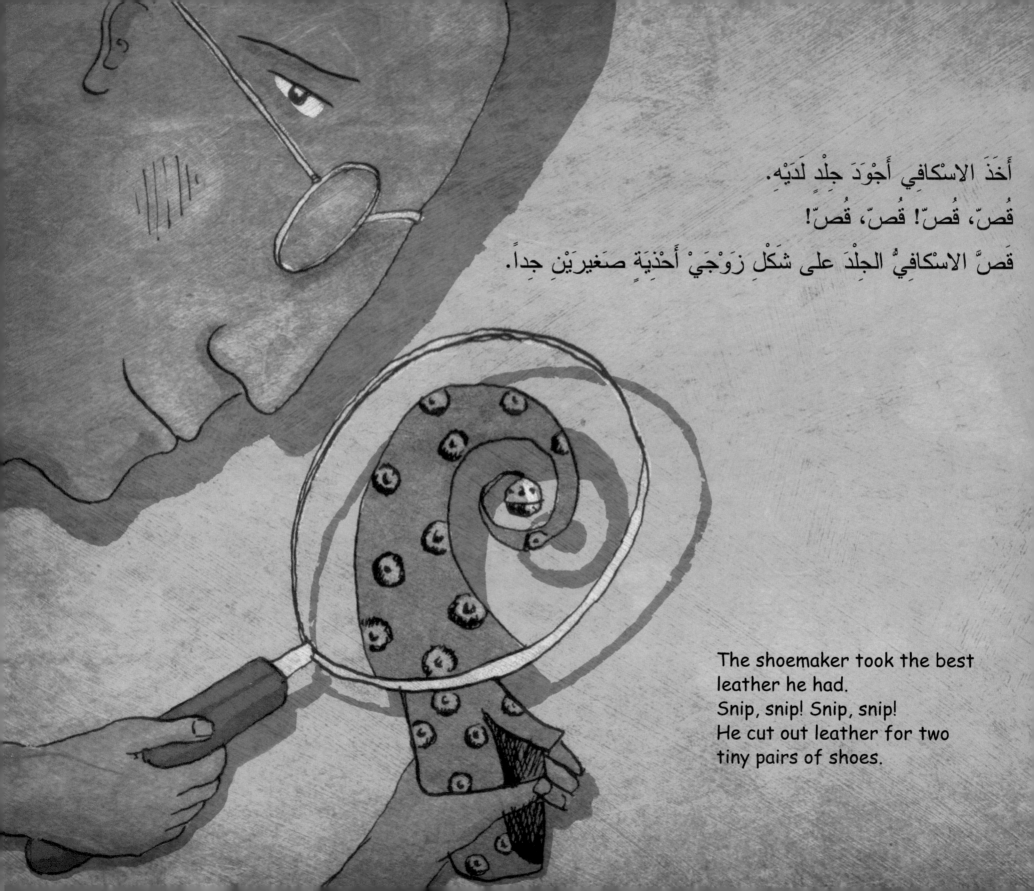

أَخَذَ الاسْكافِي أَجْوَدَ جِلْدٍ لَدَيْه.

قُصّ، قُصّ! قُصّ، قُصّ!

قَصَّ الاسْكافِيُّ الجِلْدَ على شَكْلِ زَوْجَيْ أَحْذِيَةٍ صَغيرَيْنِ جِداً.

The shoemaker took the best
leather he had.
Snip, snip! Snip, snip!
He cut out leather for two
tiny pairs of shoes.

خِطْ، خِطْ! خِطْ، خِطْ! خَيَّطَ الاسْكافِيُّ أَرْبَعَةَ أَحْذِيَةٍ صَغيرَةٍ.

طَقْ، طَقْ! طَقْ، طَقْ! دَقَّ النَّعْلَ على الأَحْذِيَةِ بِالمِطْرَقَةِ.

كَانَتْ أَجْمَلَ أَحْذِيَةٍ صَنَعَهَا في حَيَاتِه.

Swish, swish! Swish, swish! He stitched four small shoes.
Tap, tap! Tap, tap! He hammered the soles onto each pair.
They were the best shoes he had ever made.

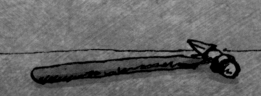  

في تِلْكَ اللَّيْلَةَ وَضَعَتْ زَوْجَةُ الاسْكافِيِّ السِتْرَتَيْنِ الصُّوفِيَّةَ والبَنْطَلونَيْنِ وَزَوْجَيْ الجَوَارِبَ عَلى دَكَّةِ العَمَلِ. وأَخَذَ الاسْكافيُّ الأَحْذِيَةَ الأَرْبَعَةَ الرَائِعَةَ المُخَيَّطَةَ بِإِتْقانٍ ووَضَعَها عَلى دَكَّةِ العَمَلِ بَدَلَ الجِلْدِ لِصُنْعِ الأَحْذِيَةِ. ثُمَّ اخْتَبَأ، هُوَ وَزَوْجَتُهُ، وَرَاءَ رُفُوفِ الدُّكَّانِ وَانْتَظَرا.

That evening the shoemaker's wife placed two jumpers, two pairs of trousers and two pairs of socks on the workbench. The shoemaker placed four perfect shoes on the workbench instead of the leather for making shoes. Then they hid behind the shelves and waited.

عِنْدَمَا دَقَّتِ السَّاعَةُ الثَّانِيَةَ عَشَرَةَ مُنْتَصَفَ اللَّيْلِ بِالضَّبْطِ ظَهَرَ الرَّجُلانِ الصَّغِيرانِ مُسْتَعِدَّانِ لِلْعَمَلِ. لَكِنَّهُمَا رَأَيَا الثِّيَابَ فَتَوَقَّفَا وَحَدَّقَا فِيهَا. ثُمَّ لَبِسَاهَا بِسُرْعَةٍ.

On the stroke of midnight the two little men appeared ready for work.
But when they saw the clothes they stopped and stared.
Then they quickly put them on.

وَكَانَا فَرِحَيْنِ جِداً وَصَفَّقَا بِأَيْدَيهِمَا طَبْ، طَبْ!

وَكَانَا فَرِحَيْنِ جِداً فَطَرَقَا بِرِجْلَيْهِمَا عَلَى الأَرْضِ طَقْ، طَقْ!

رَقَصَا حَوْلَ الدُّكَّانِ ثُمَّ خَرَجَا مِنَ البَابِ.

وَلَكِنْ... أَيْنَ ذَهَبَا يَا تُرَى لَمْ نَعْلَمْ أَبَداً.

They were so happy they clapped their hands - clap clap!
They were so happy they tapped their feet - tap tap!
They danced around the shop and out of the door.
And where they went we'll never know.

Key Words

elves	عَفَارِيتٌ صِغَارٌ	sewing	خِيَاطَةٌ
shoemaker	اِسْكَافِيٌّ	making	صَنَعَ
wife	زَوْجَةٌ	gorgeous	رَائِعَةٌ
shop	دُكَّانٌ	price	سِعْرٌ
fashions	موضة الأَزْيَاء	money	مَالٌ
shoe	حِذَاءٌ	cut out	قَصَّ
shoes	أَحْذِيَةٌ	stitch	دَرَزَ/ قَطَبَ
poor	فَقِيرٌ	day	يَوْمٌ
leather	جِلْدٌ	morning	صَبَاحٌ
pair	زَوْجٌ	evening	مَسَاءٌ
workbench	دَكَّةُ العَمَلِ	nights	اللَّيَالِي

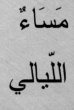

الكَلِماتُ الأَسَاسِيَّةُ:

midnight	مُنْتَصَفُ اللَّيْلِ	clapped	صَفَّقَ
stay up	سَهَرَ	tapped	طَرَقَ
hammered	طَرَقَ بِالمِطْرَقَةِ	danced	رَقَصَ
rags	ثِيَابٌ بَالِيَةٌ		
cold	بَرْدٌ		
bare	حَافٍ، عَارٍ		
sole	نَعْلٌ		
knitted	مُحَاكٌ		
jumper	سُتْرَةٌ صُوفِيَّةٌ		
trousers	بَنْطَلونٌ		
socks	جرَابَاتٌ		

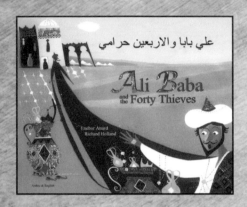

علي بابا والاربعين حرامي

Ali Baba
and the Forty Thieves

Enebor Attard
Richard Holland

Arabic & English

The books on this page have been Pen enabled.
Please touch the Pen to the left hand corner of the page for further information on language availability
or visit
www.mantralingua.com

TalkingPEN™

Неужели опять, Красная Шапочка!

Not Again, Red Riding Hood!

Kate Clynes & Louise Daykin

Ricitos de Oro y los tres ositos

Goldilocks and the Three Bears

Kate Clynes
Louise Daykin

Spanish & English

LA PETITE POULE ROUGE ET LES GRAINS DE BLE

The Little Red Hen
and the Grains of Wheat

L. R. Hen
Jago

LION FABLES
by JAN ORMEROD

三隻山羊加菲

The Three
Billy Goats Gruff

Henriette Barkow
Illustrated by Richard Johnson

Chinese & English

اللفتة العملاقة

The Giant Turnip

Adapted by Henriette Barkow
Illustrated by Richard Johnson
Arabic & English

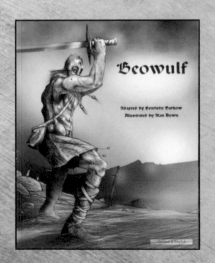

Beowulf

Adapted by Henriette Barkow
Illustrated by Alan Down

Greek & English

The Children of Lir

Oisin Casey & Diana Mayo

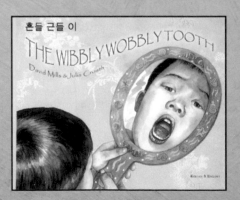

흔들 근들 이

THE WIBBLYWOBBLYTOOTH

David Mills & Julia Crouth

Korean & English